USBORNE
BOOK OF THE
SEASONS

Angela Wilkes

Edited by Felicity Brooks

Designed by
Andrea Slane and Sarah Sherley-Price

Cover and additional designs by Zöe Wray

Managing Editor: Felicity Brooks
Managing Designer: Stephen Wright
Still life photography: Howard Allman and
Amanda Heywood
Decorative borders by Kate Mawdsley
Design assistant: Katarina Dragoslavić
Photographic manipulation: John Russell
Meteorology consultant: Francis Wilson
Astronomy consultant: Stuart Atkinson

Illustrated by Dave Ashby, John Barber, Amanda Barlow, Andrew Beckett,
Joyce Bee, Stephen Bennett, Roland Berry, Gary Bines, Isabel Bowring,
Trevor Boyer, Peter Bull, Hilary Burn, Lynn Chadwick, Christine Darter,
David Eaton, Denise Finney, John Francis, Don Forrest, Victoria Gordon,
Teri Gower, Prue Greener, David Hancock, Tim Hayward, Christine Howe,
Chris Howell-Jones, David Hurrell, Ian Jackson, Roger Kent, Aziz Khan,
Kim Lane, Jonathan Langley, Richard Lewington, Kevin Lyles,
Josephine Martin, Malcolm McGregor, Doreen McGuinness,
Annabel Milne, Barbara Nicholson, Richard Orr, Lucy Parris, Julie Piper,
Maurice Pledger, Charles Raymond, Phillip Richardson, Mike Rickets, Jim
Robins, John Russell, Chris Shields, Peter Stebbing, Sue Stitt, Justine
Torode, David Watson, Phil Weare, Adrian Williams, Roy Wiltshire,
John Woodcock, David Wright, John Yates, Norman Young

Contents

4 The changing seasons
6 Skywatching
8 Why are there seasons?

Spring

10 The spring sky at night
12 Weatherwatch
14 Spring landscape
16 Roots and shoots
18 Spring daisies
20 Planting seeds
22 Pondwatching
24 Decorated eggs
26 Spring bunnies
28 Spot the babies
30 Caterpillar tracks

Summer

32 The night sky in summer
34 What's the time?
36 Tomato feast
38 Strawberry trifle
40 Summer flowers
42 Bugwatch
44 Snail trail
46 Beachcombing
48 Beach treasures
50 Harvest time

Autumn

52 The night sky in autumn
54 Everlasting flowers
56 Fruits and seeds
58 Fruity crumble
60 Autumn leaves
62 Autumn trees
64 Toadstool hunt
66 Silken webs
68 Planting bulbs
70 Chocolate cobweb cake
72 Wildlife on the move
74 Preparing for winter

Winter

76 The winter sky at night
78 Winter weather
80 Stormy skies
82 Winter buds
84 Winter trees
86 Winter flowers
88 Baked potatoes
90 Birdwatching
92 Surviving the winter
94 Useful information
96 Index

The changing seasons

In most parts of the world, the seasons change throughout the year. There are four seasons: spring, summer, autumn and winter and they follow each other in the same pattern every year. Each season is different. The weather changes and the days grow longer or shorter. In this book you can find out which special things to look out for in each season and what you can make or do.

Spring

In spring the weather becomes warmer and the days grow longer. The first flowers appear and trees burst into leaf and blossom. Spring is also the time when most birds build their nests and many animals have babies.

Summer

Summer is the warmest season of the year. The days are long and sunny and the nights are short. The trees are green and leafy and there are lots of flowers, fruit and vegetables. Animals and insects are all busy looking for food.

Baby animals, such as this Black tail deer, are born in the spring so they have time to grow strong before winter comes again.

In the summer, bees and butterflies fly from flower to flower in search of nectar.

The leaves of some trees turn yellow, red and orange in the autumn.

Autumn

In the autumn, the days grow shorter and the nights longer. It is cooler than in summer. Many trees change colour, then lose their leaves. Animals get ready for the winter ahead, stocking up on food or settling down for a long sleep.

Winter

Winter is the coldest time of the year. The days are short and the nights are long. Many places have snow and frost. A lot of trees are bare and there are very few flowers or insects around. Some animals sleep all winter long.

When it is very cold in the winter, trees are sometimes covered in a silvery coating of frost.

Skywatching

On a clear night the sky is full of stars. They look close together but they are millions of miles apart. Long ago, people noticed that the stars formed patterns or constellations in the night sky.

Star charts

Because the Earth is always moving around the Sun, we see different constellations from month to month. In this book you will find star charts for each season of the year, showing the main constellations to look out for.

Pegasus

Andromeda

Cassiopeia

To make it easier to recognize the constellations, people gave them names and made up stories about them.

You may sometimes see a meteor or shooting star.

Perseus

The white band on each map shows a faint band of stars. This is the Milky Way.

People in the southern half of the world see different stars from people in the northern half because they are looking at a different part of the sky. This is why you will find four charts for every season. Find the right star charts for where you live and follow the instructions.

Constellations

The lines joining the stars show the constellation. This is the constellation of Ursa Major, or the Great Bear. The imaginary shape of a bear is drawn around the constellation to show why it got its name.

The seven stars at the back of the bear, shown here in yellow, are also known as the Plough or the Big Dipper.

Seeing further

You can see a lot further into space if you use binoculars. You can pick out the planets, spot craters on the Moon and you may even see a comet.

Astronomers use telescopes to see thousands of times further into space.

Binoculars

Stars seen with the naked eye

The same stars seen through binoculars

The same stars seen through a good telescope

7

Why are there seasons?

The Earth is constantly spinning around the Sun. It takes a year to go around the Sun once. However, the Earth is not upright as it spins, but tilted slightly to one side. This means that whichever part of the Earth is tilting towards the Sun gets more sunlight. Because the Earth is moving, different parts tilt towards the Sun at different times of year. This makes the seasons change.

In March, neither the northern nor southern half of the Earth tilts towards the Sun. It's spring in the north and autumn in the south.

In December and January the southern half of the Earth tilts towards the Sun, so it's summer there.

It's winter in the northern half in December and January because it is tilting away from the Sun.

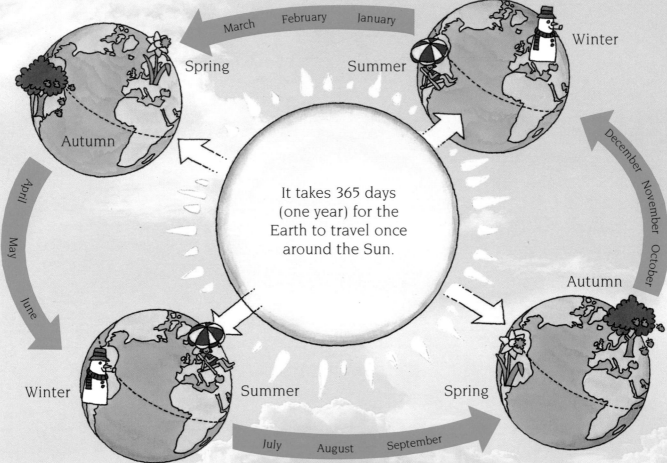

It takes 365 days (one year) for the Earth to travel once around the Sun.

In June, it's winter in the southern half of the Earth because it is tilting away from the Sun. It's summer in the northern half.

The area around the middle of the Earth has about the same amount of sunlight all year, so the seasons don't change much.

In September, neither the north nor the south is tilting towards the Sun. It is autumn in the north and spring in the south.

Spring

The spring sky at night

These star maps will help you to identify the constellations that you can see in the night sky in spring. The best time to use the maps is at around 11pm on a clear night, away from city lights.

Maps for northern half of world

The maps on this page show the stars that people in the northern half of the world can see, looking north and looking south. The names of the constellations are shown in capital letters. The only star in the sky that doesn't seem to change its position is the Pole Star, in the middle of the top map.

Look for the famous constellation Ursa Major (the Great Bear) overhead.

URSA MAJOR

AURIGA

Polaris
URSA MINOR
CORONA
BOREALIS
Capella
DRACO

PERSEUS
CEPHEUS
HERCULES
TAURUS
Algol
CASSIOPEIA
Vega
OPHIUCHUS
Aldebaran Pleiades
Deneb
CYGNUS
Rasalhague
ANDROMEDA
TRIANGULUM

West   Looking north   East

Regulus shines in the middle of the sky. It is part of the constellation of Leo (the Lion).

Castor
CANCER
BOOTES
COMA
BERENICES
LEO
Pollux
Arcturus
Regulus
GEMINI
VIRGO
Procyon
Alphard
Betelgeuse
Spica
ORION
SERPENS
HYDRA
Sirius
M42
CORVUS
CANIS MAJOR   Rigel

East   Looking south   West

Maps for southern half of world

These maps show the stars that people in the southern half of the world can see in spring. Facing north, the constellations of Pegasus and Andromeda dominate the sky. The ruby red star Aldebaran shines brightly in the east.

The most famous constellation in the skies of the southern half of the world is Crux, known as the Southern Cross. You cannot see it from the northern half of the world at any time of the year.

M31, just above the horizon, is a spiral-shaped galaxy.

Look out for the cluster of stars known as the Pleiades, or Seven Sisters, in the constellation of Taurus.

Fomalhaut

CAPRICORNUS

AQUARIUS

PISCES

CETUS

PEGASUS

ARIES

DELPHINIUS

Alpheratz

ERIDANUS

TRIANGULUM

Altair

ANDROMEDA

Pleiades

Aldebaran

AQUILA

M31

ORION

CYGNUS

PERSEUS

TAURUS

West　　　　　　　　　　**Looking north**　　　　　　　　　　**East**

Sirius is the brightest star in the sky. Canopus is the second brightest.

Fomalhaut

PHOENIX

GRUS

SMC

ERIDANUS

TUCANA

Achernar

SAGITTARIUS

DORADO

PAVO

CETUS

LMC

OCTANS

TRIANGULUM AUSTRALE

Canopus

CARINA

CRUX

Sirius

Agena

CANIS MAJOR

PUPPIS

VELA

SCORPIUS

East　　　　　　　　　　**Looking south**　　　　　　　　　　**West**

11

Weatherwatch

In spring, the weather can change very quickly. Strong winds and sudden showers are often followed by rainbows or sunshine.

You can find out how strong the wind is by looking out for signs around you. Watching the clouds can also give you clues as to what kind of weather is on the way.

Rainbows

If the sun comes out between clouds when it is raining, it shines through the drops of water and you may suddenly see a rainbow. Rainbows are always on the opposite side of the sky from the sun, so you have to stand with your back to the sun to see them. The colours in a rainbow are always in the same order – red, orange, yellow, green, blue, indigo and violet.

Red is always the colour at the top or outside of a rainbow. Violet is always at the bottom, or inside of it.

Wind speed

Weather forecasters use instruments to measure wind speed. You can estimate it by looking out for the following signs.

Calm. Smoke from chimneys rises straight up. 0-3km/h (0-2mph).

Light breeze. Smoke shows wind direction. Wind felt on face. 6-11km/h (4-7mph).

Fresh breeze. Small waves on lakes. Small trees sway. 30-39km/h (19-24mph).

Strong breeze. Hard to hold umbrellas. Big branches move. 40-50km/h (25-31mph).

Gale. Difficult to walk. Small branches broken off trees. 62-74km/h (39-46mph).

Storm. Trees uprooted and buildings damaged. 88-101km/h (55-63mph).

Cloud spotting

Clouds are made of millions of tiny drops of water. If you watch them for a while, you will see they are constantly changing shape and size. New clouds sometimes appear out of blue sky and vanish again just as quickly. Some clouds are a sign of good weather. Others show that the weather is about to change and rain is on its way.

Tall, dark cumulonimbus clouds with flat tops may bring rain and thunderstorms.

A thick layer of nimbostratus clouds blocks the sun and makes it a dull day.

Altostratus clouds form a patchy sheet of cloud that the sun can filter through.

Wispy cirrus clouds high in the sky show that wind and rain may be coming.

Large, fluffy, white cumulus clouds are usually seen on fine, sunny days.

Cirrostratus clouds form a thin film across the sky. They often bring rain.

Palm trees blowing in storm-force winds

Stratus clouds form a low layer across the sky. They can bring light rain and drizzle.

Altocumulus are small clouds all about the same size. They often lie in rows.

13

Spring landscape

As the weather gets warmer, you could try painting a spring landscape. Watercolours are good for painting skies and water, especially if you paint your picture on wet paper so that the colours run together. It is best to paint the picture in two stages, letting the colours dry in between.

You will need
Watercolour paints
Thick and fine
paintbrushes
A small sponge
Watercolour paper
A plate or palette

Painting a wash

Paint a broad stripe at the top of your paper, using a thick brush. Then quickly paint more stripes below it.

Mixing colours

1. It is best to mix watercolours on a palette. Wet your brush and dab one colour onto your palette.

2. Rinse the brush, then dip it into another colour and mix it into the first colour on your palette.

Tulips flower in the spring. Huge fields of them grow in The Netherlands.

Windmill picture

1. Wet the sponge, then use it to wet the bottom half of the watercolour paper.

2. Brush short strokes of one shade of blue across the wet paper, using a thick brush.

3. Do the same with the other blue and the green. Let the colours run together.

4. Wet the top of the paper with the sponge. Paint a pale blue wash across it.

5. Let the paint dry. Paint a broad green stripe and grey windmill shapes.

6. Paint shadows on the windmills. Use a fine brush to paint thin lines for sails.

7. Paint green leaves in the foreground of the picture, then paint red tulip flowers above them.

Roots and shoots

In the spring, new plants start to grow from seeds. You can watch how tiny roots and shoots grow by soaking bean seeds in a glass jar.

Runner beans grow from seeds.

What to do

1. Soak any labels off the jar, then rinse it out with cold water. You don't need to dry it.

2. Fold the kitchen paper or paper napkin in half. Roll it into a tube and slip it into the jar.

3. Press the kitchen paper against the sides of the jar with the handle of the spoon, as shown.

4. Peel back part of the paper. Push one of the bean seeds down between the jar and the paper.

5. Push two more beans into the jar. Spoon water onto the paper until it is really wet.

6. Stand the jar in a bright, warm place. Water it every day to keep the paper wet. Watch what happens.

The beans swell and the outer skins split. Tiny roots start to grow downwards.

Next, small green shoots uncurl and start to grow upwards. You can just see the leaves.

White rootlets grow from the roots and leaves grow.

Bean plants

Plant the plants in pots or straight in the garden. Tie them to garden sticks and water them regularly. By the end of the summer you will be able to pick your own beans.

The plants on the right are ready to be planted in pots or in a garden.

Spring daisies

You can create your own everlasting spring flowers by making them out of tissue paper. Make enough for a small posy, or arrange them in a vase.

Trace this shape to make a template.

You will need
White, yellow and green tissue paper
Tracing paper
A pencil
A pin
A paperclip
Scissors
Clear glue
A drinking straw that bends

Making a daisy

1. Trace this daisy onto a piece of tracing paper. Trace the dot in the middle. Then cut out the shape to make a template.

2. Cut out 3 squares of white tissue paper 9 x 9cm (4 x 4in). Lay them together and draw around the template.

3. Mark the dot with a pin. Remove the template and clip the paper flowers together with the paper clip.

4. Cut out the flower shapes. Fold them in half, without creasing them. Snip across the hole in the middle.

5. Unfold the petals. Fold them the other way, then snip across the hole again. Open the petals out flat.

6. Cut out a square of yellow tissue 12cm (5in) across. Make a ball of yellow paper and put it on the square.

7. Wrap the tissue paper around the ball and twist it. Hold the tail and tap the ball to flatten it.

8. Push the tail of the ball through the hole in the daisy petals. Lick your fingers and gently twist the petals to fan them out.

9. Cut out some green tissue paper 20 x 5cm (8 x 2in). Glue along one long edge, then roll the straw up in it, starting at the unglued end.

10. Dab glue around the yellow base of the daisy, then push it firmly down into one end of the drinking straw flower stem.

Arrange your spring daisies in a colourful vase or wrap them in tissue paper.

Planting seeds

Plant flower seeds indoors early in spring and they will flower in the summer. Here you can see how to grow pansies from seed but you can plant most other small flower seeds in the same way. Check the backs of your seed packets for more information.

You will need

The bottom part of an eggbox	Pansy seeds
	A sieve
Potting compost	Newspaper
A spoon	A watering can
	Flowerpots

Pansies have velvety petals.

What to do

1. Rinse the eggbox and let it drip. Half fill each section of the eggbox with potting compost.

2. Plant two seeds in each section, with a gap between them. Sieve compost on top and press it down.

3. Cover the eggbox with newspaper and leave it outside. Water the compost every few days.

4. After about two weeks, shoots will appear. Remove the newspaper so they get plenty of light.

5. When the shoots have two leaves each, pull out the smaller shoot in each section of the eggbox.

6. As the pansies grow bigger, tiny roots will begin to grow through the sides of the eggbox.

7. Soak the eggbox in water, then gently pull the sections apart. Half-fill the flowerpots with potting compost.

8. Plant a section of the eggbox in each pot. Add more compost and press it down around the plant gently.

Looking after your pansies

Put the flowerpots outside in a warm, sunny spot and water them whenever the compost looks dry. Pick off dead flowerheads and your pansies should keep flowering all summer long.

You can plant your pansies in flowerpots or straight in flowerbeds if you like.

Pondwatching

Spring is a good time to study ponds and streams because the plants are flowering and lots of small creatures live there. But take an adult with you, stay on the bank and be very careful not to fall in. If you take along a fishing net and some collecting equipment, you can take a closer look at things that live in the water.

If you are lucky, you may see a kingfisher by a pond, diving to catch fish.

Pond dipping

Here you can see what to look out for in a pond. If you have a net, sweep it gently through the water and put its contents in a jar so that you can study them. Put any plants and animals back into the pond as soon as you have looked at them.

You will need
Clean jam jars
A fishing net with a small mesh
Binoculars
A magnifying glass or hand lens
Empty plastic pots for interesting finds

Look along the banks for flowers, reeds and grasses.

Look among reeds for birds' nests, but do not disturb them.

Water lily

Water lily

Water lily

Damselfly

Moorhen chick

Look for holes in the banks where animals might live.

Look at the surface of the pond for insects, birds and plants.

Great crested newt

Stickleback

Great diving beetle

Great pond snail

In a stream, look under stones for worms, insects and leeches.

Water shrew

Looking at newts

Newts look rather like small lizards, but they are smooth instead of scaly. Like frogs and toads, they are amphibians. This means that they are born in water, but spend most of their adult lives on land. In the spring, newts head for water to find a mate and lay their eggs.

A male smooth newt shows off to a female by arching his back and flicking his tail.

Single egg

Gills

Newts lay their eggs under water one at a time, on water plants.

The tadpoles hatch from the eggs after about two weeks.

Newt tadpoles have feathery gills which they use to breathe.

Most of the newts leave the water at the end of the summer.

From tadpole to frog

Early in the spring, frogs lay their eggs, which are called frogspawn, in ponds. The tiny tadpoles that hatch do not look like frogs at first, but they change as they grow. If you keep going back to a pond where you find frogspawn, you can watch what happens.

Frogs have smooth, moist skin.

Gills for breathing

Frogs lay their eggs in clumps of clear jelly which float to the surface of a pond.

After about ten days, tadpoles wriggle out. They swim in search of food and soon grow.

The tadpoles grow legs. Now they have to come to the surface of the water to breathe.

After 12 or 13 weeks, the tadpoles have turned into tiny frogs, ready to leave the water.

Decorated eggs

Get out your poster paints, cut out some flower pictures and you can create your own collection of decorated eggs. Here you can find out how to make speckled eggs, flowery eggs and sparkling eggs. Before you decorate the eggs, you will need to blow them to empty them out. Ask an adult to help you do this. Always hold eggs very carefully, as they can break easily.

You will need

Eggs
A large needle
A small bowl
An eggbox
Poster paints
Water
Clear glue with
a fine nozzle

Paintbrushes
Scissors
Clear varnish
Flowered gift wrap
or magazine
pictures of flowers
Sequins
Ribbons

Blowing the eggs

1. Make a hole in one end of each egg with the needle. Make a bigger hole at the other end.

2. Hold the egg over the bowl. Blow hard into the small hole so that all the egg comes out of the big hole.

3. Rinse the egg under cold water. Dry it carefully then stand it, big hole down, to drain.

On farms, chicks hatch from eggs in the spring.

Speckled eggs

1. Hold an egg in one hand. Starting at one end, paint half of it with thick, pale poster paint.

2. Let the paint dry, then paint the other half the same colour in the same way. Let the paint dry again.

3. Use a stiff paintbrush to spatter the eggs first with white paint and then with brown paint.

4. When the eggs are dry, add larger dots of white and brown using a fine paintbrush.

Flowery and sparkling eggs

1. Paint the eggs with thick white or gold poster paint, one half at a time, as above, then let the paint dry.

2. Cut out flowers and leaves from the gift wrap and glue them carefully to some of the eggs.

3. To make sparkling eggs, glue sequins to some of the eggs that you have painted gold.

4. When the glue has dried, paint the eggs with clear varnish. This helps to protect them.

Group your eggs attractively and display them in pretty baskets, clear glass jars or egg boxes painted in bright colours.

25

Spring bunnies

These funny bunny faces taste like sausage rolls but look much nicer. Make them for a special spring treat. This recipe will make eight bunnies.

You will need

340g (12oz) plain flour
165g (6oz) butter
12 teaspoons cold water
115g (4oz) sausage meat
A pinch of salt
1 beaten egg
A mixing bowl
A knife
A teaspoon
A rolling pin
A round cookie cutter
A bottle top
A pastry brush
A drinking straw
A fish slice
A greased baking tray

Set the oven to 200°C/ 400°F/ Gas mark 6

What to do

1. Mix the flour and salt together. Rub in the butter with your fingers until it looks like fine breadcrumbs.

2. Add the water. Use a knife to mix the water into the flour. Squeeze the mixture into a ball.

3. Sprinkle some flour on a work surface and the rolling pin. Roll the pastry ball out thinly and evenly.

4. For each rabbit cut out three big circles and two small ones. Roll up eight small balls of pastry.

5. Brush one of the big circles with beaten egg, then put a teaspoon of sausage meat in the middle.

6. Lay one of the other big circles on top. Press your finger all around the edges to join the circles together.

Look out for rabbits in the fields in spring.

7. Brush the top circles with egg. Lift the pastry cases onto the baking tray with a fish slice.

8. Press two of the small circles onto each pastry case for cheeks. Press on a small ball for a nose.

9. Use the cookie cutter to cut out an ear from each side of one of the remaining big circles.

10. Press the ears onto the top of the pastry faces. Brush the ears, noses and cheeks with beaten egg.

11. Use the end of the straw to make eyes for each bunny. Then bake them in the oven for about 15 minutes, until golden.

Rabbits are always on the lookout, with their ears twitching and noses quivering.

Spot the babies

Spring is the season when many animals have their babies. The weather is warmer, there is plenty of food to eat and the young animals have time to grow big and strong before winter comes again. Most young animals leave their mothers soon after they are born and quickly learn how to find their own food and look after themselves.

At first, lambs just drink their mothers' milk, but after 14 weeks they start to eat grass.

Ducklings and other baby birds have fluffy down to keep them warm before their feathers grow.

Lambs

Sheep have their lambs early in the spring. Most mother sheep have one to three babies. A mother can recognize her own lambs' bleating among hundreds of others in a field.

Ducklings

Look out for ducklings bobbing along behind their mothers on ponds, rivers and lakes. Mother ducks take their new ducklings to the water's edge. The ducklings fall in and can swim straight away. When there is danger nearby, the mother duck quacks loudly and the ducklings dive underwater.

Baby birds

Birds build their nests and lay their eggs in spring. Look out for birds carrying grass, twigs or bits of fluff. This is usually a sign that they are building a nest. Once they have laid their eggs and the chicks have hatched, you may see the parent birds flying to and from the nest carrying worms or other food.

Never disturb breeding birds or their nests and eggs. It is against the law. Always watch from a distance.

A song thrush arriving back at its nest with food

Piglets

Pigs have several babies at a time. The piglets push and shove to drink their mother's milk. Newborn piglets have to look after themselves. Their mother does not clean them or help them to feed. They start eating solid food when they are three weeks old.

Piglets are curious and playful.

Fox cubs

Fox cubs are born underground in a big burrow called an earth. For the first month they stay with their mother in their earth, feeding on her milk. After that, she brings food back to the earth. By summer the cubs have started hunting on their own.

Fox cubs start to leave the earth to play when they are a few weeks old.

Caterpillar tracks

Spring is a good time to look out for caterpillars. You might spot some in a garden or out in the country. Many of them live on leaves but you may also find one wriggling across a path in search of its food plant.

Caterpillar to pupa

A caterpillar hatches from an egg laid by a butterfly or moth.

The tiny caterpillar eats and eats and grows bigger and bigger.

Then it makes a hard case called a pupa around itself.

A caterpillar has five pairs of fleshy back legs called claspers for clinging onto things.

Inside the pupa

Inside a pupa, the caterpillar turns into a butterfly (or moth). After a few weeks, the pupa skin splits and the butterfly breaks out. It stretches its wings and flies away.

Butterfly on a buddleia flower

Where to find caterpillars

Caterpillars eat leaves. Look for them both on the top and underside of leaves and grasses. Most caterpillars eat just one kind of leaf. Many of them are green, which makes them hard to spot against the leaves, but if you search carefully you may spot one.

Some caterpillars spin a tent out of silky thread and eat the leaves inside it.

The caterpillars of some tiny moths tunnel inside a leaf to eat it. Some caterpillars eat around themselves. Others move forwards as they eat.

Summer

The night sky in summer

The sky never gets really dark in summer, so only the brightest stars can be seen clearly. The best time to use these maps is at around 11pm on a clear night, away from city lights.

Maps for northern half of world

The maps on this page show the stars that people in the northern half of the world can see in summer, looking north and looking south. Looking north, the bright yellow star known as Capella hangs just above the horizon, with Regulus off to its left and the bright star Deneb high up in the east.

West   Looking north   East

East   Looking south   West

Maps for southern half of world

These maps show the stars that people in the southern half of the world can see in summer. Facing north, the easiest constellations to spot are Orion and Canis Major (the Great Dog) and over to the east you can see Leo (the Lion).

Sirius (the Dog Star), one of the stars in Canis Major, is the brightest star in the sky. Orion was a great hunter in Greek mythology and the famous constellation named after him contains many bright stars. Look out for the three stars that form Orion's belt.

LEPUS · CANIS MAJOR · PUPPIS · Sirius · ERIDANUS · Rigel · M42 · ORION · Betelgeuse · Procyon · HYDRA · CETUS · Aldebaran · TAURUS · GEMINI · Pollux · Regulus · Pleiades · Castor · LEO · PISCES · ARIES · PERSEUS · AURIGA · Capella · CANCER · TRIANGULUM

West — **Looking north** — **East**

LMC and SMC stand for Large and Small Magellanic Cloud. These are small galaxies.

PUPPIS · Canopus · VELA · CARINA · DORADO · ERIDANUS · LMC · HYDRA · Achemar · CETUS · PHOENIX · OCTANS · SMC · CRUX · TUCANA · Agena · PAVO · CENTAURUS · TRIANGULUM AUSTRALE · Fomalhaut · CORVUS · GRUS

East — **Looking south** — **West**

33

What's the time?

In summer, the days are longer and the nights shorter than at any other time of the year. Midsummer's day is the longest day of the year. The sun also rises higher in the sky than it does during the other seasons. Check to see where it rises and sets each day.

Shadow clock

You can find out how the sun changes position during the day by making a shadow clock with a friend. You will need to do this on a sunny day in a place where you are allowed to draw on the ground with chalk.

1. In the morning, ask your friend to stand with their feet together. Draw around their shoes and shadow with chalk. Then write down the time above the shadow.

2. Every two hours, do the same thing in the same spot. Write down the time above each shadow outline. Look how the position and shape of the shadow have changed during the day.

What happens

As the sun rises high in the sky in the middle of the day, shadows become shorter. As the sun moves across the sky during the day, shadows change the direction they point in because they always point away from the sun.

Shadows are longer in the morning and evening when the sun is low in the sky.

Sundials

Sundials have been used to tell the time for thousands of years. You can still see them in some places. A sundial is a very simple type of clock that uses a shadow to tell the time. Try making a sundial of your own. You will need to keep it in the same place once you have made it.

The upright part of a sundial is called a gnomon. Its shadow falls onto a flat dial marked rather like a clock face.

What time was this picture taken?

Make a sundial

You will need
A flowerpot
A ruler
A black marker pen
Modelling clay
A stick twice the height of the flowerpot

1. Turn the flowerpot upside down. Push the stick through the hole in the pot and into the ground.

2. Wedge modelling clay around the stick, as shown, to hold it upright and keep it in place.

3. Mark where the stick's shadow is by drawing a line on the pot. Write the time next to the line.

4. Do the same thing again every hour. Now you will be able to tell the time on sunny days.

Tomato feast

Home grown vegetables taste delicious and you don't even need a garden. Here you can find out how to grow tomatoes in pots. Plant them at the beginning of summer and you should have tomatoes by the end of the season.

You will need

Some small tomato plants	Small stones or gravel
Large pots	Canes
Special tomato compost	Garden ties
	A trowel
	A watering can

Tomatoes start off green and turn red when they are ripe.

What to do

1. For each plant, put small stones in the bottom of a pot. This will stop the compost from getting soggy.

2. Cover the stones with compost so the pot is about a third full. Gently tip each plant out of its pot.

3. Carefully stand a tomato plant on top of the compost in each pot. Try not to squash the leaves.

4. Fill in around each plant with more compost. Press the compost carefully so the plant stands firm.

5. Water the compost, then put the plants outside in a warm, sunny, sheltered place.

You can make a delicious salad from sliced tomatoes and mozzarella cheese, garnished with fresh basil leaves.

6. Water the plants a little every day to keep the compost damp, especially if the weather is hot.

7. As the plants grow taller and flower, carefully push a cane into each pot and tie the stem to it.

Picking tomatoes

With plenty of warmth and water, the tomatoes will swell and turn red. This means that they are ripe and ready to pick. Pick them with the stalk still on the tomato and store them in the refrigerator if you are not going to eat them straightaway.

8. If you are lucky, each flower will form a tomato. A small bunch of tomatoes is called a truss.

9. When a plant has three trusses, pinch off the top of the main stem to stop it from growing taller.

To make stuffed tomatoes, scoop out the middle of some big tomatoes and stuff them with cooked rice, peas, diced pepper and sweetcorn.

Strawberry trifle

This strawberry trifle is a lovely pudding to make for a special occasion on a hot summer's day. Try to make sure that you use the ripest, sweetest strawberries you can find and make sure you allow yourself plenty of time to prepare the trifle. Remember that you need about three hours for the sponges to go soft and you also need to allow time for the trifle to chill in the refrigerator for a few hours before you serve it.

You will need

450g (1lb) fresh strawberries
6 trifle sponges
2 tablespoons strawberry jam
4 tablespoons apple juice
1 small lemon
300ml (½ pint) double cream
3 tablespoons milk
Half a teaspoon vanilla extract
2 tablespoons caster sugar

Serves four

38

What to do

1. Rinse the strawberries under a cold tap, then cut around the stalks and cores with a small knife and pull them out.

2. Cut most of the strawberries in half, but leave a few whole ones. Put the halved strawberries in a big glass or china bowl.

3. Cut the sponges in half. Spread each half with jam then press them together again. Cut the sponges into quarters.

4. Put the pieces of sponge on top of the strawberries and mix them together. Sprinkle the apple juice over the top of them.

5. Cover the bowl with cling film. Put it in the fridge for about three hours, until the sponges have gone soft.

6. Grate the yellow skin (the zest) from the lemon, using the small holes of a cheese grater. Scrape the zest off with a knife.

7. When the sponge mixture has chilled, pour the cream into a large bowl. Add the milk, lemon zest, vanilla and sugar.

8. Beat the mixture with a whisk for several minutes until it becomes thicker and forms floppy peaks. It shouldn't be too stiff.

9. Spoon the whipped cream over the sponge mixture and spread it out. Refrigerate the trifle until you are ready to serve it.

Summer flowers

By pressing flowers you can keep them for a long time and use them on pictures and cards. The easiest to press are open-faced flowers, such as pansies, or bell-shaped ones. Press flowers as soon as you pick them, so they do not wilt, and always ask permission first.

Pressing flowers

You will need
Common or garden flowers, such as pansies, fuchsias and primulas
Heavy books
Blotting paper

1. Pick fresh, undamaged flowers that have fully opened. They should be dry, not wet with rain or dew.

2. Put paper on one side of an open book. Lay flowers on it so they are flat and not touching.

3. Lay another piece of paper on top of the flowers. Smooth it down carefully, then close the book.

Pressed fuchsia flowers

4. Stack more books on top. Leave the flowers in the book for four weeks, to dry and flatten out.

Making pictures

You will need
Thick paper or thin cardboard
Scissors and glue
Cotton buds
Clear plastic film

1. Cut out pieces of thick paper or cardboard for the bases of your pictures, gift tags or bookmarks.

2. Lay pressed flowers and leaves on each piece of card and paper. Try out different arrangements.

3. Dab a tiny dot of glue on the back of each flower and leaf, then stick them down in position.

4. Cut out pieces of plastic film bigger than the cards. Cover the cards with the film and trim the edges

Seasonal flowers

Summer is a good time to press flowers because there is a wide variety to choose from, but of course you can also press them in the spring and even the autumn. Be very careful when you handle any pressed plants, as they are very delicate and break easily.

Flower picture

Arrange pressed flowers, leaves and ferns on a piece of thick, textured paper. You could arrange them to look as if they are growing naturally, or make a pattern with them.

Bookmark

Use a narrow strip of thin cardboard to make a bookmark. This shape works best with small delicate flowers and leaves.

Gift tags

To make gift tags, glue the pressed flowers and leaves onto small pieces of thin cardboard. Punch a hole in each tag and thread a ribbon through it to attach it to the gift.

A picture, bookmark and gift tag, all decorated with pressed flowers, leaves and ferns

Bugwatch

In summer, you only have to turn over a stone, dig up some soil or look at any plant to come across countless insects and other tiny creatures. They are all around you in gardens, fields and woods, ponds and streams and on the seashore. Watch what they do and you can learn a lot about how animals live.

A bumblebee gathering nectar and pollen from a flower

Bees

Bees feed on nectar, a sweet liquid found inside most flowers. Most bees gather nectar from one type of flower at a time. As a bee flies from flower to flower, it also gathers pollen, the sticky yellow dust inside flowers. It carries the pollen to other flowers and this helps the flowers to make new seeds.

Dragonflies

Look out for dragonflies flying low above ponds and streams early in the summer. Their brightly coloured bodies flash as they swoop across the water, chasing insects. You may see them rest on leaves, their wings outstretched in the sun.

Peacock butterfly

Butterflies

Butterflies and moths are attracted to brightly coloured, scented flowers. Like bees, they feed on nectar. Watch how they stretch out a long, thin tube called a proboscis as soon as they land on a flower. They use this proboscis like a drinking straw to suck up the sweet nectar.

Close-up of a butterfly's head and proboscis

Dragonflies have four gauzy wings.

42

Ants

Ants live together in enormous groups called colonies. They make nests by burrowing in sand or soil. If you watch where a line of ants goes, you will probably find their nest hole. The ants work hard, carrying food and other things back to their colony. They leave a scent trail between the food they find and the nest, so that the rest of the ants know which way to go.

Wood ants carrying food back to their nest

Dung beetles gather animal dung and roll it into a ball. They eat some of it and lay eggs in the rest.

Beetles

Beetles have hardened front wings that protect their delicate flying wings. Look for them under bark and stones or around rubbish heaps. They eat all kinds of plants and animals. There are thousands of different beetles living everywhere. See how many you can find.

Beetles are the most heavily armoured of all the insects.

Devil's coach horse beetle

Green shield bug

In the soil

If you dig around in the soil, you may find grubs or larvae. These are baby insects. Many insects, such as beetles and flies, lay their eggs in the soil. When the larvae hatch, they stay under the ground and eat the roots of plants. Some larvae stay under the ground for several years before they change into insects and go up above the ground.

Insects and their larvae

Cranefly

Cockchafer beetle

Click beetle

Dot moth

43

Snail trail

Snails live in damp, shady places and are quite easy to find. They usually hide during the day. Look for them in cracks in walls, inside empty flowerpots or under big stones.

Snails slither along the ground, leaving a trail of slime behind them. The slime helps them to cling onto things and to move over sharp surfaces without hurting their feet.

A snail has two pairs of tentacles. It smells with one pair and has eyes on the other pair. When disturbed, it pulls its tentacles in and may even vanish into its shell.

These long tentacles have eyes at the ends.

African Giant Snail

Young African Giant Snail

Snails may cluster together in a hiding place.

The snail smells and feels things with these short tentacles.

Hiding away

Snails often hide together in the same place. They find their way there by following their slime trails. If you find snails in the same spot, mark their shells carefully with a waterproof pen. Go back every day to check how many of the marked snails are there.

Garden snails

Snail shells

Shells protect snails' soft bodies. Baby snails have soft shells which harden as they grow. If you look at a snail's shell, you can see lines. The distance between them shows how much the snail has grown in a year.

Snail enemy

Some birds, such as thrushes, eat snails. They pick up a snail in their beak and smash the shell against a stone so they can eat the snail inside. Bits of shell are left around the stone.

A thrush breaks a snail's shell by smashing it on a stone.

How snails move

To see how snails move, put one inside a glass jar. Look at its foot and you will see ripples pushing it forward.

Snail eggs

In the summer you sometimes find snails slithering over each other. This means they are mating. Afterwards, each snail lays its eggs in a hole in the soil. Look out for clusters of round, white eggs buried just beneath the soil.

A snail and its eggs

Feeding habits

Snails usually come out to feed at night, or after rain. This is because their skin isn't waterproof and they die if they dry out. In winter, or in hot weather, snails hide in shady spots. They close themselves into their shells with slime which sets into a hard seal. Most snails feed on plants and are especially fond of soft growing shoots.

Snails eat by filing off bits of leaf with rows of tiny teeth on their tongues.

Snails feed on soft growing shoots.

Beachcombing

If you go to a beach, you can have fun looking for shells, pebbles and other treasures. It is best to explore at low tide when the sea is right out. Try looking along the line of seaweed that marks high water level at the top of the beach.

Collecting shells

You will find shells on most beaches. They were made by tiny animals which lived inside them. When the animals died, their shells were left behind and washed ashore. Only collect empty shells. If you pick up a shell with an animal in it, put it back where you found it.

Shells come in many shapes and sizes. Gastropods are single shells and are often coiled. Bivalves come in pairs, joined by a little hinge. See if you can find any of the shells shown here.

How to collect

1. Use buckets or plastic bags for collecting shells. Label the bags to say where you found the shells.

2. When you get home, soak the shells in warm, soapy water. Gently scrub them clean with an old toothbrush.

3. Some shells come in pairs. Wrap some thread around them to keep them together while they dry.

4. Store fragile shells on cotton wool in a box. Display the others on a tray or a box lid.

Spider conch

Cat's paw scallop

Prickly cockle

Wentletraps

Cone shells

Oysters

Top shells

Violet sea snails

Tiger cowrie

Moon shells

Serpent's head cowries

Calico clam

Jingle shells

Venus clams

Coquina clams

Beautiful tellin

Limpets

Razor shells

Watermelon tellins

Queen scallops

Mussels

Common whelks

Abalones

Pebbles and other finds

Look for interesting stones along rocky beaches. Pebbles come in many colours and sizes, depending on the rock they are made of. You may find pieces of coloured glass that have been worn smooth by the sea. On some beaches you may find interesting bits of driftwood, or even some fossils.

This fossil ammonite shows the shape of the animal's shell.

Fossils

Fossils are the remains of animals that lived many millions of years ago. Very slowly, as the years went by, their remains turned to stone.

Fossils in limestone

Sea glass

Driftwood

Calcite vein

Flints

Seaweed

Starfish

You might find a starfish washed up on a rocky beach. Starfish usually have five arms which are covered in small bumps and have suckers underneath.

Common starfish (below) are orange. Spiny starfish (right) are purple or brown.

Pebble made of marble fragments

Quartz veins

Beach treasures

There are lots of things you can do with the treasures you have collected from the beach. You could make a display tray to show them off, create attractive paperweights or decorate boxes and picture frames.

Display tray

You will need
A large pizza box
Newspaper
A craft knife
Thin white cardboard

Used matchsticks
Felt or coloured paper
A pen
Sticky tape

1. Fill the pizza box with crumpled newspaper. Tape the lid shut. Tape round the corners of the box as well.

2. Glue coloured paper or felt to the top and sides of the box. Cut several pieces and join them neatly.

3. Arrange your collection on the box. Mark several dots around the edge of each object with a pen.

4. Remove the objects from the box. Carefully cut a tiny cross over each dot, as shown, with the craft knife.

Use the display tray as a showcase for your collections of fossils, pebbles or seashells.

5. Push a matchstick into each hole, with the used end down. Leave about 1cm(½in) of each matchstick showing.

6. Put the objects back, so the matchsticks hold them in place. Make a card label for each object.

Decorating things with seashells

Lid decorated with shells that have been glued one on top of another.

Shells glued to a picture frame

You will need
Different-shaped seashells
Box lids, picture frames or hair clips
PVA glue
Clear varnish
A paintbrush

1. The surface you want to decorate must be clean and dry. Arrange some shells on top of it.

2. Glue on the shells. Pick up one shell at a time, dab glue on it, and press it in place.

3. When the glue has dried, paint the shells with varnish. Let it dry, then paint a second coat.

Funny face pebbles

Use small shells to decorate a plain hairclip or hairband.

Keep unpainted pebbles in water to make them look bright.

Painted pebbles

You will need

Large, smooth pebbles
Poster or acrylic paints
A thick paintbrush
A thin paintbrush
Clear varnish

Cat paperweight

Patterned paperweights

1. Wash each pebble and let it dry. Paint it all over with a thick coat of white paint and let it dry.

2. Paint the pebble with whichever colour you want to use as your base. Let the paint dry again.

3. Paint a picture. Do the outlines first and let them dry. Then add details with a fine brush.

4. When the paint has dried, paint a coat of varnish over it and let it dry. This protects the paint.

Harvest time

Many different kinds of food and drink are made from plants. Fruit and vegetables come from plants, but so do other everyday foods, such as flour, coffee, cocoa, cooking oil and sugar. Most plant foods are grown as crops and are picked or harvested in the summer.

Grain crops

Look out for combine harvesters working in fields late in the summer. These huge machines harvest crops such as wheat, oats, rye and barley that are grown for their seeds or grain. Combine harvesters don't just cut the crop, they also gather it together and separate the grain from the stalks. The grain is ground into flour or used to make breakfast cereals.

Sunflower seeds are in the middle of the flowers.

Sunflowers

In some countries with warm climates, sunflowers are grown as a crop. The sunflower seeds are harvested and used to make cooking oil.

Cherries

Strawberries and raspberries

Maize

Maize is a tall leafy plant grown for its plump yellow cobs of grain. Most maize is grown for animal feed, but it is also used to make cooking oil, breakfast cereals and popcorn. Some sweet varieties are sold as corn on the cob.

Soft fruits

Soft fruits are ripe and ready to pick in the summer. They are sometimes grown on farms where people can go and pick the fruit themselves.

Corn on the cob

Gooseberries

Blackcurrants

Autumn

The night sky in autumn

These star maps will help you to identify the constellations that you can see in the night sky in autumn. The best time to use the maps is at around 11pm on a clear night, away from city lights.

Maps for northern half of world

Facing north, look out for Ursa Major which is below the Pole Star and parallel with the horizon. Looking south, you should be able to see Pegasus (the Winged Horse), which has a square of stars in the middle. The single star Fomalhaut flashes just above the horizon, and to the east Altair shines brightly.

Vega
CEPHEUS
CASSIOPEIA
ANDROMEDA
Algol
PERSEUS
Polaris
URSA MINOR
DRACO
Capella
Pleiades
HERCULES
AURIGA
Aldebaran
CORONA BOREALIS
URSA MAJOR
TAURUS
BOOTES

West — Looking north — East

This is the best time to see M31, a huge, distant galaxy. It is just visible with the naked eye.

M31
ANDROMEDA
Alpheratz
Deneb
CYGNUS
TRIANGULUM
PEGASUS
ARIES
DELPHINIUS
PISCES
Altair
AQUARIUS
AQUILA
Rasalhague
CETUS
CAPRICORNUS
OPHIUCHUS
Fomalhaut

East — Looking south — West

Maps for southern half of world

Looking north, a triangle of three bright stars dominates the sky: Regulus, which is blue, yellow Arcturus and blue-white Spica. Also look for the constellations of Virgo (the Virgin) and Leo (the Lion).

Looking south, the Milky Way crosses the sky in a wide band. Crux (the southern Cross) is almost overhead. Above it is Centaurus (the Centaur). A centaur was a mythical creature that was half man and half horse.

LMC and SMC stand for Large and Small Magellanic Cloud. These are small galaxies.

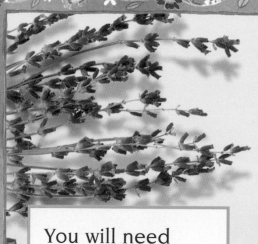

Everlasting flowers

In the autumn, you can use dried flowers and leaves to decorate your home. Look out for interesting plants that are drying out naturally, seed heads, bracken, reeds and grasses.

You will need
A strong elastic band for each type of flower
String
Scissors

Drying flowers

Good flowers to dry are statice, sea thistles, strawflowers, lavender, love-in-a-mist and poppy seed heads. Choose flowers that are almost fully open, and pick them with long stems. Always ask an adult before you pick anything.

1. Pick the flowers on a dry day, once any dew has dried. Sort each type of flower into a separate bunch.

2. Strip the lower leaves off the stems. Fasten each bunch of flowers together tightly with an elastic band.

3. Fan the flower heads out a little so that they aren't touching each other. This stops them from rotting.

4. Hang the bunches upside down in a cool, airy place away from direct sunlight, such as a garage or shed.

Lavender, statice, strawflowers and dried poppy seed heads

Leave the flowers until they have dried out completely. Handle them carefully when you take them down as they will be quite delicate and may snap easily.

Dried flowers look good packed into baskets or jugs, so that you can see the flowers but not the stems. Try different arrangements to see what looks best.

Preserving leaves

You can preserve autumn leaves with glycerine (from a pharmacy). They will darken a little, but still look fresh and natural. Choose large sprays of tree leaves in different colours.

You will need
A sharp knife
Glycerine
Hot water
A measuring jug
A large spoon
A jug or large jar
String

1. Mix 300ml (¹/₂ pint) glycerine with 900ml (1¹/₂ pints) hot water in a jug or a large jar.

2. Ask an adult to help you cut a slit about 5cm (2in) long at the end of each stem of leaves.

3. Put the branches in the jug. If they drink a lot of the mixture, make more and top it up.

4. When the leaves begin to darken, take them out of the jar and tie them together with string.

5. Hang the leaves upside down in a dark, dry place. Leave them until they have dried out completely.

Arrange the dried leaves in a big jug or vase to create a dramatic effect.

Fruits and seeds

In late summer and autumn, trees produce seeds. Some come in nuts, others are encased in juicy fruits or tucked away in cones. In fact, all these things are fruits and do the same job. They protect the seeds inside and help them spread to a new place where they can grow. See how many of these different kinds of tree seeds you can find.

Seeds

Rowan

Fruit

The seeds of broadleaved trees

Broadleaved trees all produce seeds inside fruits. These may be hard nuts, berries or soft fruits.

Nuts have hard outer shells. These have to break or rot before the seeds inside them can start to grow into new trees.

Sweet chestnut

Fruit

Edible seed

Fruit

Seeds

Fig

These fruits contain seeds.

Ash fruits have wings. These spin in the wind to carry the seeds away.

Soft fruits and berries are eaten by birds and animals. They drop the seeds inside the fruits, spreading them to new places.

Conifer seeds

Conifers are trees that produce their seeds in cones. Most cones have woody scales that open in warm, dry weather to release the seeds. The scales close when it is wet.

Norway spruce

Stone pine

Cone scale

Wing

European silver fir

Larch cones sometimes stay on a tree for many years.

European larch

Cones are many different shapes and sizes.

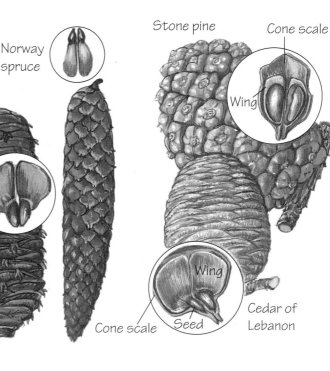
Wing

Cone scale

Seed

Cedar of Lebanon

Seed bracelet and necklace

Look out for interesting large tree seeds and flower seed heads that you can collect to make into a necklace or bracelet.

Bracelet

1. Choose the seeds you want and lay them out in the order or pattern you want to use them.

3. Carefully pierce each seed in turn with the needle, then thread it onto the elastic. Tie the ends together.

2. Cut a piece of shirring elastic long enough to go around your wrist. Thread the elastic onto the needle.

You will need
Large seeds and seed heads
Strong thread
Scissors
Large needle
Shirring elastic

Necklace

1. Thread the seeds onto a length of strong thread long enough to make a necklace.

2. When all the seeds are threaded, tie the ends of the thread together in a knot.

This necklace is made of small fir cones sprayed gold, poppy seed heads, senna pods, sunflower seeds and pumpkin seeds.

Fruity crumble

You can use most kinds of fruit for this wonderful pudding with a crunchy crumble topping. It is very good made with apples, but you could also make it with half apples and half blackberries, or use other autumn fruits, such as plums or pears.

What to do

1. Peel the apples, cut them into quarters and cut out the cores. Slice them and put them in the pie dish.

2. Add the apple juice or water, the cinnamon and caster sugar and stir everything together well.

3. Sift both types of flour into a mixing bowl. Cut the butter into small cubes and add it to the bowl.

4. Rub the butter into the flour with your fingertips, lifting the mixture and letting it fall back into the bowl.

5. When the mixture looks like coarse breadcrumbs, add the brown sugar. Mix this in with your hands too.

Plums, apples and blackberries all make excellent crumbles.

Try making crumble with different types of apple, to see which you like best.

6. Spread this crumble mixture over the apple and press it down firmly with a fork. Put the dish on a baking tray.

7. Put the crumble on the middle shelf of the oven and bake for 35 to 40 minutes, until the topping is golden brown.

8. Push the tip of a knife into a piece of the apple. If it's not soft, put the crumble back into the oven for five more minutes.

Serving the crumble

When the crumble has cooked and the apple is soft, take it out of the oven and leave it to cool for 10 to 15 minutes before you serve it. Fruit crumbles are delicious served warm with custard, pouring cream or a dollop of vanilla ice cream. Any leftover crumble tastes good reheated or eaten cold the following day.

Warm fruity crumble with vanilla ice cream

Autumn leaves

In the autumn, the leaves of many trees fall to the ground. Trees that lose their leaves like this are called deciduous trees. Most of them have soft, flat leaves. These often change colour before they fall, and turn red, yellow, orange or brown. Here you can find out how to press autumn leaves to keep in a scrapbook and how to make leaf prints.

English oak
(rounded lobes)

Field maple
(jagged)

Common lime
(heart-shaped)

Leaf shapes

Leaves are many different shapes and sizes. Some are a simple shape. Others are split into several parts, have zigzag edges or rounded lobes. All trees breathe and feed with their leaves. The green colour in the leaves makes food from air and water while the leaves are in daylight.

Leaves in close-up

The upper surface of a leaf is tough and often glossy to stop the sun from drying it out. If you look closely at the underside of a green leaf, you will see a network of tiny veins running through it.

Autumn leaves. From the left, clockwise: Red oak, Copper beech, Ginkgo, Rowan, Common pear.

Close-up, showing the veins on the underside of a leaf

Changing colour

In autumn, it is not warm enough for soft leaves to make much food. A corky layer grows across the leaf stalk, cutting off the water supply to the leaf. The leaf changes colour, dries out and dies.

Make a leaf scrapbook

You will need
Autumn leaves
Sheets of blotting paper
A heavy book
A heavy object

1. Lay the leaves between sheets of blotting paper, so they don't touch. Put the book and weight on top.

2. After a few weeks the leaves will be flat and dry. Tape them into a scrapbook and label them.

If you find skeletons of old leaves, put them in a scrapbook too.

Leaf prints

You will need
Different shaped leaves
Poster paints
Thick paper
Scrap paper

1. Paint an even layer of paint over the underside of a leaf. Start at the middle and paint outward.

2. Gently lay the leaf paint-side down on the paper. Put scrap paper over the top and press it firmly all over.

3. Lift off the scrap paper, then carefully peel off the leaf. Use the tip of a knife to do this if it is difficult.

4. To make more delicate prints, print the leaf again three or four times without adding any more paint.

5. Make prints of different leaves in red, orange and yellow to create a striking autumn leaf picture.

Autumn trees

As the trees change colour in the autumn, try drawing a picture of them with chalk pastels. These are good for drawing landscapes because they are soft and blend together easily. Pastels work really well on coloured paper. For the best results, use thick paper with a textured surface.

You will need
Coloured sugar paper or textured paper
Chalk pastels

Mixing colours

You can mix pastels straight on your paper by drawing strokes of one colour across strokes of another colour.

Experiment with different combinations of colours and shades.

Blocking

Use the side of a pastel to create blocks of colour. Then go over them with blocks of different colours.

Try different shapes, colours and patterns.

Hatching

Use the end of a pastel like a pencil to draw short diagonal lines. Then draw more short lines over them in different colours.

Blending

To create a softer effect, try drawing overlapping strokes in different colours.

Then gently smudge them together with the tip of your finger, or you could use a cotton bud.

Autumn landscape

1. Block in the sky, with a turquoise chalk pastel. Leave a blank area of paper for the trees.

2. Add patches of pale blue to the sky. Then block in small patches of dark blue over the top.

3. Block in the shapes of different coloured trees with yellow, orange and rust pastels.

4. Hatch over each tree with darker or contrasting colours. Let the colours blend together.

5. Block in stripes of green, yellow and orange to look like a field in the foreground.

6. Hatch across the stripes with orange and brown. Make the stripes longer in the foreground.

7. Use a black pastel to draw a line below the trees, then draw the tree trunks and branches.

Toadstool hunt

Early autumn is the best time to go hunting for toadstools and mushrooms. You can find an astonishing variety in woods and meadows, and even in gardens. All toadstools and mushrooms are fungi. These are plants that don't have any leaves or flowers but send tiny threads down into other plants or animal dung and feed on them. Some fungi grow among dead leaves; others grow on tree trunks or dead logs. Here are some to look out for.

Warning
Some toadstools are edible, but others that look similar are deadly poisonous. Do not pick toadstools unless you are with an adult, and never taste or eat toadstools you find.

Fly agaric toadstools look pretty but are actually poisonous.

Fairy ring toadstools
Often grow on lawns in a ring. The ring grows larger every year as the toadstools' underground threads reach out into fresh soil for food.

Cep
Edible. Has a dark brown cap with pores underneath, rather than gills. Usually grows under conifers.

Fly agaric
Poisonous. Usually grows under birch or pine trees, often in sandy soil.

Stinkhorn
Has a nasty strong smell. Grows in woods and hedgerows.

Wood blewit
Has a lilac tinge. Grows in woods.

Birch bracket
Has a creamish brown cap that splits with age, and white spores. Grows on birch trees, which it kills.

Dryad's saddle
Has a pale yellow-brown cap with darker scales. Grows on the trunks of broad-leaved trees.

Honey fungus
Has cream-coloured gills that turn brown with age. Grows at the base of trees, which it eventually kills.

Crimson wax cap
Grows in grass fields and along roadsides. Colour of the cap fades with age.

Parasol
Has white gills and a scaly cap. Grows in woods and grassy places.

Field mushroom
Usually grows in fields or grassy road verges. It has a pale brown cap and dark brown gills.

Chanterelle
Edible. Has fold-like ridges and smells of apricot. Grows in broad-leaved woods, especially beech and oak.

Giant puffball
One of the biggest fungi. Splits open when ripe. Grows in fields, woods and hedgerows.

Common puffball
Covered with small bumps. Grows in woods.

Silken webs

The best time to see spiders' webs is early on an autumn morning, when their fragile threads are strung with beads of dew or mist. Spiders spin webs to catch insects. Different spiders build different types of web. Here are some to look out for.

Spiders use special organs in their abdomens to spin their silk threads.

Orb webs

Garden spiders build orb webs. First, a spider spins a framework. Next, it spins spokes across the framework. It joins the spokes together with spirals of special sticky thread.

Spiders often build a new web every day, as webs are easily broken or damaged. You may find an old web with holes in it, or areas that a spider has repaired.

The spider lies in wait in its web, or hides under leaves, joined to the web by a thread. When an insect flies into the web, the web shakes and the spider rushes out to attack.

Spiders move across their webs very fast when the web shakes.

Sometimes spiders wrap a fly up in thread before eating it.

Garden spider hiding

Sheet webs

House spiders spin sheet webs in the corners of rooms. Insects can't escape the fine threads.

Tube webs

The wall spider spins a tube-like web in cracks in walls. It pulls unwary insects down into the tube.

Nursery webs

One kind of wolf spider spins a web like a tent around her eggs. She tears it open when the baby spiders hatch.

Money spiders

These tiny spiders spin fine webs like hammocks across a lawn. The webs sometimes blow away in the wind.

Web sketches

Go on a web hunt one morning and make sketches of them. Look carefully at them but do not touch them as you will break the fine threads.

You will need
Sheets of black paper or card
A fine silver felt pen or gel pen

1. First draw the framework of the web that runs around the outside. Then add the spokes that go into the middle.

2. Next draw the inside pattern. If it is a spiral, start in the middle and work carefully out to the edge.

No two webs look exactly the same.

Planting bulbs

Many spring flowers grow from bulbs, but you have to plant them in autumn, 8 to 12 weeks beforehand. You can plant them in a garden, or in pots. You can also plant them in indoor pots, as long as you keep them in a cool, dark place for two to three months. Indoor bulbs flower earlier than outdoor ones because it is warmer inside.

Crocuses

Daffodils

You will need
A large, frost-proof pot with drainage holes in the bottom
Gravel or pebbles
Potting compost or bulb fibre
Bulbs, such as narcissi, tulips, crocuses or dwarf irises
A stick

Outdoor pots

1. Put a layer of gravel in the pot, then fill two thirds of it with compost. Make a hole for each bulb.

Crocuses are some of the first bulbs to flower.

2. Put each bulb in a hole with the pointed end facing upwards. The bulbs must not touch each other.

3. Fill the pot with compost so the bulbs are buried twice as deep as their own height. Put the pots outside.

Growing bulbs indoors

Good indoor bulbs are hyacinths, amaryllis, dwarf irises and narcissi, such as "Paper white" and "Tête-à-tête". Plant hyacinths early in the autumn to flower in the winter.

A hyacinth flowers after 12-15 weeks.

1. Put gravel and bulb fibre or compost in a pot as above. Don't fill the pot to the top.

2. Gently press a bulb into the middle, pointed end up. Fill in compost around the edges.

3. Stand the pot on a saucer. Water the compost around the bulb, to make it moist.

4. Put the bulb in a cool, dark place for 8 to 10 weeks. Keep the compost damp.

5. When the leaves have grown as tall as your first finger, stand the pot in a light, cool place.

6. When the plant has grown a little more, put it in a warm, light place and a flower will grow.

Growing hyacinths in water

You can also grow hyacinths in water, without any soil, and watch their roots and leaves grow. You can either grow them in a special hyacinth jar, or suspended in a jar with cocktail sticks. It is best to wear gloves when you handle the bulbs, as they can give you a rash.

You will need
Rubber gloves or old gloves
A hyacinth bulb
3 cocktail sticks
A glass jar or hyacinth jar

Special hyacinth jar

1. Nearly fill the jar with cold water. Wearing gloves, push the sticks into the fattest part of the bulb.

2. Rest the cocktail sticks on the rim of the jar, so that the fat end of the bulb is just above the water.

3. Put the jar in a cool, dark place. Once the roots have grown, move it to a warm, light place.

Chocolate cobweb cake

Make this delicious cake for an autumn party or celebration. It is very easy because all the ingredients are mixed together in the same bowl. Remember to allow time for the cake to cool before you ice it.

You will need

For the cake:
2 rounded tablespoons cocoa powder
4 tablespoons hot water
225g (8oz) soft margarine
225g (8oz) caster sugar
4 eggs
175g (6oz) self-raising flour
55g (2oz) ground rice

1 level teaspoon baking powder

Two 20cm (8in) sandwich cake tins

For the icing:
225g (8oz) plain chocolate
115g (4oz) butter
55g (2oz) white chocolate

Oven temperature:
180°C/350°F/
Gas mark 4

Making the cake

1. Set the oven. Grease the two cake tins and line each one with a circle of greaseproof paper.

2. Put the cocoa powder in a bowl. Slowly stir in the hot water, to make a smooth paste.

3. Put all the other cake ingredients in a mixing bowl. Add the cocoa mixture then beat everything together well.

4. Pour half the mixture into each tin. Bake the cakes for 25-30 minutes, until they have risen and are firm.

The cake is really chocolatey inside. It serves about 14 people.

5. Run a knife around the edges of the cakes, then turn them out onto a wire rack to cool.

Icing the cake

1. Break the plain chocolate into a small bowl. Stand it over a pan of water over a low heat.

2. Cut up the butter and add it to the bowl. Stir the butter and chocolate until they have melted.

3. Sandwich the cakes together with half of the icing. Spread the rest over the top and sides.

4. Break the white chocolate into a bowl. Stand it over a pan of hot water and stir it until it melts.

5. Let the chocolate cool for five minutes. Spoon the chocolate into one small plastic bag inside another.

6. Hold the bag over a plate and snip off a tiny corner. Be careful not to let the chocolate run out.

You use dark and white chocolate to make patterns in the icing.

7. Gently squeeze the bag to draw a circle on top of the cake. Draw more circles around it.

8. Pull a skewer from the centre of the cake to the edge several times to make a pattern.

Serving the cake

Once you have iced the cake, leave it for a while to let the icing set before serving it. The cake tastes best the day you make it, but it will keep for several days as long as you keep it in an airtight tin.

You can make a different pattern by piping straight lines across the cake and then dragging a skewer across them.

Wildlife on the move

As the days grow shorter and colder in autumn some birds and animals leave their summer homes and travel great distances to spend the winter in warmer lands where there is plenty of food. This is called migration. In spring, they return to their breeding grounds.

In the autumn, Arctic terns fly from the Arctic to the Antarctic, at the other end of the world.

A long march

Reindeer and caribou live in the far North, near the Arctic Circle. In the winter, it is hard for them to reach the plants they eat buried beneath the snow and ice, so enormous herds of animals travel thousands of kilometres south in search of food. If they didn't do this, many of them would die.

A line of migrating caribou may stretch for 300km (186 miles). Caribou are good swimmers so they can cross rivers on the way.

Butterfly travellers

Most butterflies don't survive the winter, but some of them migrate to warmer countries. In the autumn, thousands of Monarch butterflies flock together and set off on an epic journey from Canada all the way to the Gulf of Mexico.

Monarch butterfly

Monarch butterflies settle down to roost when the temperature drops below a certain level. These are on a tree trunk.

Birds that fly in flocks often have striking markings that help the rest of the flock to recognize them.

Migrating birds

At the end of the summer, huge flocks of swallows gather on overhead wires before taking off on flights of 9,700km (6,000 miles) from Europe to southern Africa. Swallows eat insects, which are only plentiful in the spring and summer.

Caribou follow the same migration routes every year. They can walk across deep snow because their wide hooves are fringed with fur, like snow-shoes.

Swallow

Swallows have to fly all the way across the Sahara Desert on their journey south. There is hardly any water in the desert, so they fly non-stop. They live on food and water stored as fat under their skin.

Hoopoes fly from Europe to Africa every autumn.

Finding the way

Nobody is entirely sure exactly how birds find their way over such long distances. Birds that fly in the daytime may follow landmarks, such as rivers and mountains, or may find their way by the position of the Sun. Birds that fly at night may use the stars and moon to help them navigate.

Preparing for winter

In the autumn, wherever you live, you may spot signs of birds and animals getting ready for the winter. Many of them stock up on food before it becomes scarce; others are preparing shelters or homes to keep them warm and safe for the winter.

European jay with an acorn picked from an oak tree

Arctic fox in thick, white winter coat

Storing food

In autumn, jays collect acorns from oak trees and bury them. They dig them up in the winter when they need food. Squirrels also bury nuts to eat later on in the winter. They eat seeds, cones and fruit too. They often have a favourite feeding place, such as a tree stump and scatter shells and leftovers around it.

Grey squirrel burying nuts in the autumn. Any nuts that a squirrel forgets about may sprout and grow into trees.

Winter coats

Many mammals, such as foxes, grow longer, thicker winter coats. This helps them to keep warm as the weather becomes colder.

Wild corner

You can help animals to find food and shelter for the winter by creating a wild corner in a garden. Let the grass and weeds grow, to encourage insects and butterflies.

Fungi and mosses grow on rotten wood. Insects live in it, providing extra food for birds.

Leave fallen fruit for birds and animals to feed on.

Butterflies and bees are attracted to autumn flowers, such as michaelmas daisies which are rich in nectar.

Winter

The winter sky at night

These star maps will help you to identify the constellations that you can see in the night sky in winter. The best time to use the maps is at around 11pm on a clear night, away from city lights.

Maps for northern half of world

Facing north, look for Ursa Major balancing on its tail and Cygnus (the Swan). Looking south, winter is the best time to see Orion, one of the brightest constellations, high in the night sky. Orion contains several brilliant stars, including Betelgeuse, which is reddish in colour, and Rigel, which is blue-white.

PERSEUS
CASSIOPEIA
Alpheratz
CEPHEUS
Polaris
URSA MINOR
PEGASUS
Deneb
URSA MAJOR
DRACO
LEO
CYGNUS
Vega

West   **Looking north**   **East**

Winter is a good time to look for shooting stars, especially in mid-December.

Capella
AURIGA
Algol
PERSEUS
ANDROMEDA
Castor
GEMINI
TAURUS
Pleiades
TRIANGULUM
Pollux
Aldebaran
ARIES
CANCER
Betelgeuse
ORION
Procyon
M42
Rigel
Regulus
HYDRA
Sirius
CETUS
PISCES
Alphard
CANIS MAJOR
ERIDANUS

East   **Looking south**   **West**

Maps for southern half of world

There are plenty of bright stars to look out for at this time of year. Try to spot Deneb, Arcturus, Spica, Altair, Vega and Fomalhaut. Looking north, the easiest constellations to spot at this time of the year are Aquila (the Eagle), Capricornus (the Sea Goat) and Sagittarius (the Archer). The Milky Way is seen at its best here, cutting the sky in half. Looking south, it runs through Crux (the Southern Cross) and Centaurus (the Centaur).

LMC and SMC stand for Large and Small Magellanic Cloud. These are small galaxies.

Winter weather

In most parts of the world, winter is colder than the other seasons. The days are also shorter and the nights longer. In countries where the temperature drops below freezing point for much of the winter, there is a lot of frost and snow. In some places there may be snow on the ground for several months.

Icicles form when it is so cold that drips of melting snow freeze.

Every snowflake is different but they all have six points.

Frost

On cold, dry winter's nights there is often a frost. Freezing cold surfaces are covered with a fine layer of ice crystals. Rime is white frost that forms when an icy wind blows over grass and trees. Each branch and blade of grass is coated with a furry layer of ice crystals.

If you live in an area where it snows, you can make a snowman.

Snow

When it is very cold, it may snow. The tiny drops of water in clouds freeze into ice crystals that join together to make snowflakes and flutter to the ground. For snow to settle, it has to be cold enough for it not to melt once it reaches the ground. Snowflakes are so small you can only see them properly under a microscope.

Snowshaker

Make a model snowman inside a jar,
then shake it to create your own snowstorm.

You will need
White, brown, red and green modelling
clay
Silver glitter
A jam jar with a screwtop lid
Thin silver wire
Glycerine (available at a pharmacy)
Blue food colouring

1. Make a snowman
on a mound out of
the clay. It must be
small enough to fit
inside the jar.

2. Push the model
snowman firmly
onto the inside of
the jar lid, so that it
sticks in place.

3. Twist a piece of
thin wire into a bare
tree shape. Stick it
into the "snow" next
to the snowman.

4. Half fill the jar
with glycerine. Pour
in enough water to
make the jar three
quarters full.

5. Pour quite a lot
of silver glitter into
the jar, then add a
couple of drops of
blue food colouring.

6. Lower the model
slowly into the jar.
The liquid will rise
to fill the jar. Screw
on the lid tightly.

7. Dry the outside
of the jar, then turn
it the right way up
and watch the snow
flutter down.

Shake the shaker to make it snow.
The glycerine in the water helps
make the snow fall gently.

You can use any model that the
water won't spoil. This is a model
of a house on a hill.

Stormy skies

Watercolours are very good for painting moody skies and clouds, especially if you wet the paper first. Before you start a picture, try some of the ideas shown below to find out how to create different effects. You only need three colours for the picture. It's a good idea to try mixing them first, to see how many different colours you can make.

You can buy watercolours in tubes or pans.

You will need
Watercolour paints
A thick paintbrush
A small sponge
Tissues
Watercolour paper
A plate or palette

Mix yellow and blue to make green.

Mixing greens

Mix yellow and blue together. Then mix in small amounts of burnt umber to make different shades of green.

A thundery sky

Wet the paper. Paint a wash of mid blue (see page 14), then paint a wash of dark blue over the top half of it.

Painting clouds

1. Wet the paper and paint a blue wash over it. To make clouds, dab off patches of paint with a tissue.

2. If you want to make the clouds look like rain clouds, add a darker colour along the bottom of each cloud.

As a finishing touch, you could add some flying birds to your stormy sky painting.

Stormy sky picture

You will need to use three different watercolour paints for this stormy sky picture: Prussian blue, yellow ochre and burnt umber. If you don't have these colours, use whichever shades of dark blue, yellow and brown that you do have.

1. Wet a sheet of watercolour paper all over, using the small sponge or thick paintbrush.

2. On your palette or plate, mix Prussian blue with burnt umber to make dark grey.

3. Dab large patches of dark grey paint onto the top part of the paper with your paintbrush.

4. Clean your brush, then add patches of yellow ochre to the dark grey, so they run together.

5. Mix three or four different shades of green and dab them over the bottom part of the paper.

6. Build up the patches of green so they run into the grey paint, to create a rainy effect.

7. When the sky has dried, paint a castle with the same dark grey paint you used for the clouds.

81

Winter buds

In the winter, trees hardly grow at all, but slow down and rest. Most broadleaved trees have no leaves in winter, but they all have buds containing the baby leaves, shoots and flowers for the coming spring. The winter buds and twigs of different trees may look different, but they all have the same basic features.

Winter twigs

On the right is a three-year-old horse chestnut twig. Its buds have sticky scales. They grow opposite each other in pairs. The leading bud holds next year's shoot. It is covered with thick scales that protect it from the cold and insects. The new stem and leaves are inside the scales.

Flower head

Bud scales

Leaf

Cross-section of a horse chestnut bud

Leading bud

This side bud will grow into a twig if the leading bud is damaged.

A leaf scar left by last year's leaf

Last year's leading bud was here and left a girdle scar. You can tell how old a twig is by counting how many girdle scars it has.

This side shoot grew from a side bud. It is two years old.

These side buds will grow into leaves.

Leading bud

Last year's buds were here.

The twig above is from a two-year-old Norway spruce. The spruce is an evergreen, so does not lose its leaves each winter.

Horse-chestnut sticky buds

Forcing buds

You can 'force' some buds to open in the winter, sooner than usual, by cutting some twigs and bringing them indoors. Some twigs to try forcing are forsythia, horse chestnut, birch and willow. Stand the twigs in a vase or glass jar in a sunny spot, then wait for the buds to open.

Spotting winter buds

If you look carefully at winter buds and twigs, you can spot the differences between them. This will help you to identify which tree they come from. Check to see if the buds grow in opposite pairs, or singly - first one side of the twig then the other. Look at their colour and shape. Are the buds covered with scales or furry hairs? If there are scales, how many and are they sticky? Here are some common twigs to look out for.

Ash
Smooth, grey twig. Large, black opposite buds.

Sycamore
Large, green opposite buds with dark-edged scales.

False acacia
Grey twig. Thorns next to tiny, alternate buds.

Beech
Slender twig. Alternate, spiky brown buds that stick out.

English elm
Zigzag twig with alternate dark red twigs.

Common lime
Zigzag twig. Alternate, reddish buds with two scales.

Willow
Slender twig. Alternate buds lying close to twig.

Common alder
Alternate, stalked purple buds, often with male catkins.

Walnut
Thick, hollow twig. Big, black alternate buds.

White poplar
Twig and alternate buds covered with white down.

Turkey oak
Clusters of alternate buds with whiskers.

Sweet chestnut
Knobbly twig. Large, reddish alternate buds.

Wild cherry
Clusters of large glossy red buds at tip of twig.

London plane
Alternate, cone-shaped buds. Ring scar around bud.

Magnolia
Huge, furry, greenish-grey buds.

Whitebeam
Downy, green alternate buds.

Winter trees

Each type of tree has its own special shape, depending on the shape and size of its trunk and the way its branches grow. You can see the shapes of trees best in the winter, when many of them lose their leaves. This gives you a good chance to see their branches properly.

Deciduous trees

Trees that lose their leaves in winter are called deciduous trees. They nearly all have broad, flat leaves. Deciduous trees lose their leaves every autumn, then grow new ones the following spring.

Copper beech

Horse chestnut

Field maple

English oak

Evergreen trees

Evergreen trees keep their leaves all the year round. Most of them have long, thin leaves called needles, which have a hard, waxy surface. Some of them have tiny scale-like leaves that overlap each other.

Silver birch trunks

Corsican pine

Norway spruce

Blue Atlas cedar

Lawson cypress

Tree spotting

Look out for different trees when you are out in a park or the countryside in winter. Making quick sketches will help you to remember what they look like. When you get home, compare your sketches with the pictures here, or look them up in a book.

Hawthorn

London plane

Horse chestnut

Monkey puzzle (Chile pine)

Judas tree

Looking at bark

Another way to recognize winter trees is to look at their bark. This is the tough outer layer of the trunk that protects a tree from disease. When a tree is young, its bark is smooth and thin. As the tree grows older, its bark gets thicker and forms different patterns.

Silver birch bark peels off in strips that look like ribbons or wood shavings.

The bark of an English oak tree has deep ridges and cracks.

A beech tree has smooth, thin bark that flakes off in tiny pieces.

The bark of the Scots pine flakes off in large pieces.

Winter flowers

Few plants flower in the winter, because frost and ice harm them. But towards the end of the winter, when it starts to get warmer, the first flowers appear. Look out for them in sheltered spots in gardens, parks or woodlands.

Snowdrop

Christmas rose

The first flowers

Clumps of snowdrops with their tiny nodding flowers appear in late winter once any snow has melted. They grow from tiny bulbs.

Winter aconite

Winter aconites grow in sheltered flower beds and under trees. The small, yellow flowers appear in the late winter and early spring.

Christmas roses flower in the middle of winter, in shady, frost-free spots. The plant has dark, waxy evergreen leaves which can stand the winter cold.

Winter squills can be found in rock gardens at the end of the winter. The green leaves appear first, followed by the blue, bell-like flowers.

Winter squill

Glory of the snow

Glory of the snow have small, star-shaped blue and white flowers. They grow in flower beds and rock gardens. The flowers open when the winter snow is melting.

Pasque flowers are bell-shaped.

Crocus

Pasque flowers and crocuses come out at the end of the winter. The flowers only open when it is warm and sunny. If the sun goes in, they close their petals. You can find yellow and white crocuses as well as purple ones. Each colour flowers at a slightly different time.

86

Winter-flowering shrubs

At the end of the winter, these shrubs flower in sheltered places, adding a burst of colour to the wintry landscape.

Winter jasmine (below) is often trained to grow up walls. The yellow trumpet-shaped flowers appear first, followed by small, glossy leaves.

Winter jasmine

Female flowers

Viburnam tinus

Stamens that make pollen

Viburnum tinus is a bushy evergreen shrub with pointed oval leaves. The heads of pinkish-white flowers have a sweet smell.

Exotic camellia flowers appear at the end of the winter. The flowers can be red, pink or white and grow on shrubs with dark, glossy leaves. Camellia flowers can be damaged by frost, so they only grow well in mild, frost-free places.

Catkins

Some trees have two kinds of flowers that appear late in the winter in places with a mild climate. One kind of flower is female and makes seeds. The other type is male and makes pollen. The male flowers are called catkins and grow in clusters on long stalks.

Leaf bud

These male flowers make pollen. Lots of them grow together on a long stalk called a catkin.

Catkins come out in late winter or early spring before the leaves open. The wind blows them about and the pollen drifts away on the breeze.

Look for camellias in woodland and city gardens.

Baked potatoes

Baked potatoes are one of the easiest things to cook and make a warming meal on a winter's day. Below are two suggestions for different fillings - tuna and sweetcorn or cheese and pickle, but you can use any filling you like. The quantities given for the fillings here are both enough to fill two potatoes. Set the oven at least 20 minutes before cooking the potatoes, to give it enough time to warm up.

You will need

2 large baking potatoes
Vegetable oil
Butter or margarine

For the tuna filling:
200g (7oz) can tuna
1 tablespoon mayonnaise
200g (7oz) can sweetcorn

For the cheese filling:
85g (3oz) cheese
Pickle

Oven temperature:
200°C/400°F/Gas mark 6

1. Set the oven. Hold the potatoes under running cold water and scrub them clean with a small brush.

2. Prick the potatoes all over with a fork. Rub them with vegetable oil and put them on a baking tray.

3. Put the tray of potatoes on the top shelf of the oven. Cook them for an hour, then take them out.

4. Test the potatoes with a small knife to see if they are cooked. They should feel soft all the way through.

5. If still hard, cook them for another 15 minutes, then test them again. If they are soft, cut them in half.

6. Put a little butter or margarine into each potato. Then spoon in the filling you have chosen.

Baked potatoes filled
with tuna and sweetcorn
(left) and cheese and pickle (right)

Tuna and sweetcorn filling

Pile the filling
onto the potato.

1. Open the cans of tuna and sweetcorn with a can opener. You may need to ask an adult to help you.

2. Drain the liquid from each can by holding down the lid and tipping it upside down over the sink.

3. Put the drained tuna into a small bowl. Mix in the mayonnaise and two tablespoons of sweetcorn.

Cheese and pickle

Try fillings of butter,
or soured cream
and chives.

Grate the cheese onto a plate. Put half the cheese in each potato, then spoon a little pickle on top.

Birdwatching

It is hard for birds to find enough to eat in the winter, so you can help them by putting out food and water for them in your garden or on a window ledge. This gives you a good opportunity to watch them at close hand.

Meadowlark

Putting out food

These are foods that different birds like to eat. You can also buy wild birdseed from pet shops. Don't feed the birds in the breeding season in spring, as baby birds need natural food, such as insects and grubs.

Bread

Cheese

Bacon

Banana

Dried fruit

Cooked potato

Food chart

	WORMS	SNAILS	INSECTS
Blackbird			
Song thrush			
Robin			

Scatter food on the ground for birds such as thrushes and blackbirds.

Hang up a net bag filled with unsalted nuts, or thread peanuts in their shells onto string.

To find out which foods birds like, make a chart showing what different birds eat.

Make a bird bath so the birds have water to drink and wash in. Change the water every day to keep it clean.

Feeding time

Watch birds quietly, without disturbing them. Make notes of what they look like, or do quick sketches, to help you identify what they are.

If you have a bird table, scatter food on the table and hang nuts or bird pudding from hooks around the edges.

90

Making bird pudding

You will need
A yogurt pot
String
A big needle
Cooking fat
Breadcrumbs, oats and cooked potato

1. Thread the yogurt pot onto the string. Fill it with the cooked potato, breadcrumbs and oats.

2. Ask an adult to melt the fat. Pour it into the yogurt pot and mix it with everything else.

3. Leave the fat to set hard. Then hang the pot upside down from the piece of string.

Plants for birds

The plants shown below attract birds to a garden because they provide food. Shrubs and trees that produce berries in the autumn, such as rowan, crab apple, elder, and holly, are valuable sources of natural food for many birds.

Hawthorn

Groundsel

Rowan

Cotoneaster

Elder

Thistle

Wild grasses

Female bullfinch on sunflower seedhead

Do not cut the seed heads off teasles, sunflowers and thistles in the winter as finches and other birds will feed on any seeds that are left. You can also put sunflower seeds out on your bird table.

A blue tit drinking water from a dripping garden tap

Blackbird on ivy

Ivy climbs up walls and trees and is used as a nesting site by many birds. Its berries provide food in the winter.

Surviving the winter

Different animals have different ways of coping with the cold weather and lack of food in winter. Some of them go to sleep or hibernate all winter until spring comes. Others have thick coats to keep them warm, so they can carry on looking for food throughout the winter.

Bats hibernate in hollow trees, caves or lofts. They sleep hanging from their claws, upside down.

The big sleep

Some animals stock up on food during the autumn, so they are well fed at the start of the winter. Then they burrow into their shelters and fall fast asleep. They don't eat all winter long. By the time spring comes, they are much thinner and need to find food.

Alpine marmot

Hedgehogs curl up in a ball and hibernate for five months in a nest of grass, moss and leaves.

Alpine marmots

Alpine marmots seal themselves into their burrows under the ground and sleep for the winter, that is for six months of the year. When they are asleep, their body temperature drops and their heartbeat slows down so they can survive until the spring without food.

Entrance blocked with earth and stones

Marmots hibernating

Chamber for droppings

Winter in the den

Bears do not hibernate, as their bodies do not slow down in the winter, but they shelter in their dens and doze. Female polar bears give birth to up to three cubs at a time in dens in the snow, where they are safe from the freezing winds outside. The cubs stay in the den for about three months, feeding on their mother's milk. The mother eats nothing herself. She just rests.

Hole for air

Main chamber

Cubs' chamber

Entrance tunnel

Some dens have a lower chamber too.

Changing coats

Many Arctic and mountain animals which don't hibernate change the colour of their coats at different times of the year. In the winter, their coats or feathers are white, making it hard to see them against the snow. In the summer, when the snow has melted, their coats are grey or brown, so they blend in with the surrounding rocks and plants. This camouflage makes it hard for both hunters and prey to see each other.

Snowshoe hare in winter coat

Arctic fox in winter coat

Snowshoe hare in summer coat

Ptarmigan in summer

Arctic fox in summer coat

Ptarmigan in winter

Hibernating insects

Some insects spend the winter in hiding places, without moving or feeding. You may find them on tree trunks, under stones, in the corners of houses and sheds, in wood piles or among dead leaves. Note where you find them, but do not disturb them.

Moths often rest on bark of tree trunks, especially if they are the same colour as the bark. Look in cracks in the bark and you may find pupae.

Green lacewing

Peacock butterfly

If you search the corners of a shed or outhouse in winter, you may be able to find a butterfly or a lacewing hibernating.

Above you can see some of the many different insects that like to hibernate in sheltered spots such as woodpiles in the winter.

Useful information

Equipment

You don't need special equipment or materials for most of the activities in this book, but there are some things you might find useful.

Watching animals

For many of the nature activities in this book it is a good idea to have a pair of binoculars and a hand lens or magnifying glass. A good pair of binoculars when you are starting out is either 8x30 or 8x40 (The numbers tell you how strong and what size the binoculars are). Make sure they are light and comfortable to hold and ask an adult to show you how to focus them.

Other things that may be useful for watching animals are a notebook and pencil (for doing quick sketches or making notes), plastic bags and containers for collecting things, a small camera, string, labels and a small rucksack to carry everything in.

Gardening things

Go to a garden centre or a big supermarket with a gardening section to buy everything you need for gardening, such as plant pots, potting compost, bulbs and seeds. Ask for help if you can't find what you want. The backs of seed packets give you all the information you need for planting seeds. Bulbs are usually only available in late summer and early autumn, just before you should plant them.

Art equipment

You can buy watercolour paints, pastels, pencils, paintbrushes, different sorts of paper and craft materials at art shops, large branches of stationers, or in good department stores. Look for boxes of paints and pastels that are specially made for children, as they are usually cheaper. Watercolour blocks are more economical to use than tubes. You don't need to buy a proper palette to mix paints, just use an old plate, or the lid from a plastic container.

Looking after nature

When you go for a walk or take part in a nature activity, take care of the countryside and its wildlife and make sure you stay safe.

- Always tell your parents or carers where you are going and what you plan to do.

- Do not drop litter. Take your rubbish home with you.

- Keep to paths and close gates behind you.

- Leave things in the wild as you found them. Do not damage any plants or trees.

- When collecting things, only take what you need and make sure you leave plenty of specimens behind.

- Never disturb nesting birds or take birds' eggs.

- Be gentle with any creatures you catch, however small. Study them gently then put them back where you found them.

- Only pick wild flowers if there are plenty growing and only pick a few. Never uproot a plant or pick rare flowers.

Activity tips

- Before you start, cover your work table with newspaper, unless you can wipe it clean. Put on an apron or old shirt and roll up your sleeves.

- Read the instructions before you begin and gather together everything you need.

- Be very careful with sharp knives and scissors.

- Never use a cooker unless there is an adult there to help you.

- When cooking, wear oven gloves when picking up or moving any hot dishes or pans.

- When you have finished, clear up any mess you have made.

Finding out more

If you want to find out more about animals and plants, write to the following organizations. Some of them have special wildlife clubs and magazines for children.

Wild animals

Go Wild! Club, WWF,
Panda House,
Weyside Park,
Godalming,
Surrey, UK GU7 1XR
Web site: www.wwf-uk.org/

Insects

The Bug Club
AES
PO Box 8774
London, UK SW7 5ZG

Mammals

The Mammal Society,
15 Cloisters House,
8 Battersea Park Road,
London, UK, SW8 4BG
Web site: www.mammal.org.uk/

Birds

RSPB Wildlife Explorers
(formerly called YOC),
RSPB Youth Unit,
The Lodge,
Sandy,
Bedfordshire, UK, SG19 2DL
Web site: www.rspb.org.uk/

Trees

The Woodland Trust,
Autumn Park,
Dysart Road,
Grantham,
Lincolnshire, UK MG31 6LL
Web site: www.woodland-trust.org.uk/

Plants

Plantlife,
21 Elizabeth Street,
London, UK, SW1 9RP.
Web site: www.plantlife.org.uk/

Web sites to visit

The Really Wild Show (BBC TV nature programme): www.bbc.co.uk/reallywild/

Kids Ark: web.ukonline.co.uk/conker/

All About Birds:
www.zoomschool.com/subjects/birds/

The sea and the sky:
www.seasky.org/sea.html/

Heavens above (information on skywatching): www.heavens-above.com/

Index

ammonite, 47
amphibians, 23
animals, 4, 22, 23, 28-29, 56, 72-73, 74, 92-93
ants, 43
apples, 58, 59
Arctic fox, 93
astronomers, 7
autumn, 5, 8, 51-74

baby animals, 4, 28-29
baked potatoes, 88-89
bark, 43, 85, 93
bats, 92
beach, 46, 47, 48
beachcombing, 46-47
beans, growing, 16-17
bears, 92
bees, 5, 42, 74
beetles, 43
berries, 50, 56
binoculars, 7
bird pudding, 91
bird table, 90, 91
birds, 29, 56, 72, 73, 90-91
bivalves, 46
blending colours, 62
blocking colours, 62, 63
bookmark, making a, 41
buds, 82-83
bugs, 42-43
bulbs, planting, 68-69
butterflies, 5, 30, 42, 72, 74, 93

cake, chocolate cobweb, 70-71
caribou, 72-73
caterpillars, 30
catkins, 87
chicks, 24
chocolate cobweb cake, 70-71
clocks, shadow, 34, 35
clouds, 12, 13, 80, 81
cooking,
    baked potatoes, 88-89
    chocolate cake, 70-71
    fruity crumble, 58-59
    spring bunnies, 26-27
    strawberry trifle, 38-39
cones, 56, 74
conifers, 56
constellations, 6, 7, 10, 11, 32, 33, 52, 53, 76, 77
crocuses, 68
crops, 50
crumble, fruity, 58-59

daffodils, 68
daisies, paper, 18-19
deciduous trees, 60, 84
dragonflies, 42
ducklings, 28

Earth, 6, 8
eggs, 23, 29, 30, 43
    blowing, 24
    decorating, 24-25
evergreen trees, 82, 84

flowers, 37, 40-41, 42, 68, 69, 82, 86-87
    drying, 54-55
    paper, 18-19
    picture, 41
    pressing, 40-41
food for birds, 90-91
fossils, 47, 48
fox cubs, 29
frogs, 23
frogspawn, 23
frost, 5, 78, 86
fruity crumble, 58-59
fruits, 50, 56, 74
fungi, 64-65, 74

gardening, 20-21, 36-37, 68-69
gardens, 42, 74, 90-91
gastropods, 46
gift tags, making, 41
gills, 23
gnomon, 35
grain crops, 50
growing seeds, 16-17
grubs, 43

hare, snowshoe, 93
harvest, 50
hatching colours, 62, 63
hibernating, 92, 93
hoopoes, 73
hyacinths, 69

icicles, 78
icing, 70, 71
insects, 42-43, 66-67, 74, 93
ivy, 91

jay, 74

kingfishers, 22

lambs, 28
landscapes, 14-15, 63

larvae, 43
leaves, 5, 17, 30, 60-61, 64, 82, 84
    preserving, 55
    printing, 61

maize, 50
marmots, 92
meteor, 6
migration, 72-73
Milky Way, the, 6
mixing colours, 14, 62, 80, 81
moths, 30, 42, 43, 93
mushrooms, 64-65

nectar, 42, 74
needles, evergreen, 84
nests, 29, 43
newts, 22, 23
night sky, 6-7, 10-11, 32-33, 52-53, 76-77
nuts, 56, 74

painting, 80, 81
    pebbles, 49
    a spring landscape, 14-15
    a stormy sky, 80-81
    a wash, 14
paints, 14, 15, 24, 25
pansies, 20, 21
paper flowers, 18-19
paperweight, 49
pastels, 62, 63
pastry, making, 26-27
pebbles, 46, 47, 49
picture, 40, 41
    leaf, 61
    stormy sky, 80-81
    windmill, 15
piglets, 29
plants, 16, 17, 18, 19, 22, 23, 45, 50, 54, 64, 65, 68, 69, 86-87, 91
polar bears, 92
pollen, 42, 87
ponds, 22-23, 42
potatoes, baked, 88-89
proboscis, 42
ptarmigan, 93
pupa, 30

rabbits, 2, 6, 27
rain, 12, 13
rainbows, 12
reindeer, 72-73
roots, 16-17

seasons, 4-5, 8, 34
scent, 43
seed heads, 54, 57, 91
seeds, 42, 56-57, 74, 91
    growing, 16-17
    planting, 20-21
shadow, 34, 35
shadow clock, 34
sheep, 28
shells, 44, 45, 46, 48, 49
shooting star, 6
shoots, 16-17, 45, 82
shrubs, 87
sketches, 67
sky, 6, 10-11,
snails, 44-45
snow, 78, 79
snowshaker, 79
soil, 43
spiders, 66, 67
spring, 4, 8, 9-30,
    bunnies, cooking, 26-27
squirrels, 74
stamens, 87
starfish, 47
star maps, 6, 10, 11, 32, 33, 52, 53, 76, 77
stars, 6-7,
strawberry trifle, 38-39
stuffed tomatoes, 37
summer, 4, 8, 31-50
sun, 6, 8, 12, 34
sundial, 35
sunflowers, 50, 91
swallows, 73

telescope, 7
tentacles, 44
thrush, 45
time, telling the, 34-35
toadstools, 64-65
tomatoes, 36-37
trees, 56, 60, 82-83, 84-85
    drawing, 62-63
trifle, strawberry, 38-39
tulips, 14, 15
twigs, winter, 82-83

watercolours, 14-15, 80-81
weather, 4-5, 12-13, 78-79
webs, 66-67
wind speed, 12
windmill picture, 15
wings, 42, 43
winter, 5, 8, 74, 75-93

Every effort has been made to trace the copyright holders of the material in this book. If any rights have been omitted, the publishers offer to rectify this in any subsequent edition, following notification. The publishers are grateful to the following for permission to reproduce material:

Cover: Tree © Richard Hamilton Smith/CORBIS; p4: Black tail deer and young © Darrell Gulin/CORBIS; p5: Frost-covered trees © Digital Vision; p9: Chick and eggs © Stockbyte; p13: Clouds © Digital Vision; Palm trees © Douglas Peebles/CORBIS; pp14-15: Tulip field © Digital Vision; p16: Painted Lady runner bean © Photos Horticultural; p24: Chick and eggs © Stockbyte; p26: Adult cottontail rabbit © W. Perry Conway/CORBIS; p27: Young eastern cottontail rabbit © Lynda Richardson/CORBIS; p28: Ducklings © Julie Habel/CORBIS; p29: Piglets © Julie Habel/CORBIS; p29: Fox cubs © Manfred Danegger/Still Pictures; p31: Sunflowers © Digital Vision; p34: Yellow tulips and shadows © Michael S. Yamashita/CORBIS; p35: Sundial © The Purcell Team/CORBIS; p50: Combine harvester © Julian Calder/CORBIS, Summer fruits © Michelle Garrett/CORBIS; p51: Fly agaric toadstools © Digital Vision; p60 and 61: Autumn leaves © CORBIS Digital Stock; p62 and 63: Autumn leaves © CORBIS Digital Stock; p64-65: Fly agaric toadstools © Digital Vision; p67: Spiders' webs © Uwe Walz/CORBIS; p75: Snowflake © Jim Zuckerman/CORBIS; p78: Snowman © Stockbyte, Icicles © CORBIS Digital Stock, Snowflakes © Jim Zuckerman/CORBIS; p82: Horse chestnut buds © Sally A. Morgan; Ecoscene/CORBIS; p84: Silver birch trees © CORBIS Digital Stock; p85: Snow scene © CORBIS Digital Stock; p86: Camellias © The Purcell Team/CORBIS; p91: Blue tit and ivy © John Watkins; Frank Lane Picture Agency/CORBIS; p92: Pipistrel bat hibernating in cave © Tim Wright/CORBIS; All background photographs © Digital Vision